Silence of the Song Trees

Branwen OShea

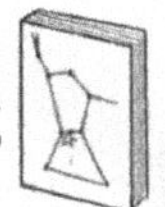

Sigma Orionis Publishing

For the trees and all those

who hear their songs...

ONE

Cerulean perched on a mid-branch of the grand tree, waving his tail in rhythm with the ethereal overtones of the song trees and the voices of his fellow Firth. His mouth, however, was full of sweet bon fruit, so he hummed along, hoping no one would notice. He'd entered his first growth spurt, and his need for constant snacks seemed endless. The perfectly ripened bon fruit exploded in his mouth, spraying its creamy juice over his soft-scaled arms and the branch.

From her neighboring perch, his friend, Hematite, snorted. The crescendo of other voices nearly drowned out her tinkling laughter. Blushing, he lapped the excess juice off his arms and apologized to the tree. It rumbled back in amusement.

Not wanting to shirk his responsibility to the trees any longer, Cerulean swallowed the remaining sweet pulp and joined in the refrain. He opened his palm to get rid of the sticky, damp fruit pip, but the branches below him were full of other iridescent Firth, glowing their unique colors among the long, spiraled leaves. *If I drop a pip on someone's head, they'll definitely know I've been eating and not singing.* Giggling at his predicament, he wrapped his webbed fingers around the gross, sticky pip and dove fully into the music.

Cerulean loved this morning ritual. Since the dawn of time, the Firth had united their voices with the ancient song trees to balance their shared planet, Lenglood. He and his fellow Firth were as intertwined symbiotically with the song trees as the notes they sang together every dawn. As the sun rose higher, the overtones of the trees transformed into lyrics, singing out to all of Lenglood, connecting them in a harmonious symphony. Deep inside himself, somewhere below his double hearts, Cerulean settled as the symphony drew to a close. A lovely sense that all was well, his knot secure in the web that united his lovely planet, filled him.

The first playful call of "Remember us," drifted down from the highest tree branch. A moment later, that fellow Firth disappeared. One by one, with a sound like the wind in the rushes, the youngest Firth gleefully popped out of physical existence.

His hearts racing, Cerulean kept his gaze on the grasses below, plotting out his morning strategy. Epic games required epic strategy, and he was not going to let Hematite, Clay, or whoever else was *it* catch him today.

He leaned left and then right, straining to spot any telltale movement on the forest floor. But given his high perch, the thick branches, long leaves, and shifting mist made it difficult. None of his brightly-colored peers had reappeared immediately below the tree, but the green-toned ones might simply be too well camouflaged to see from this height.

Tapping his toes against the bark in excitement, he waited his turn. Usually, their sacred loch was his best hiding spot, since his namesake cerulean light blended with the blue waters, but that was the first place everyone searched for him.

From above him, Clay, called, "Remember us." With a wink at Cerulean, Clay shifted, disappearing only to reappear probably somewhere reddish-brown, like his glow. A moment later,

Hematite whooshed away. Cerulean waited for three heartbeats then shifted himself.

For a brief moment, he was on another plane of Lenglood, identical to the physical one, except in the alternate one, everything glowed, not only the Firth. Beautiful, geometric lines of light pulsed between everything, connecting their spirits.

He shifted again, appearing near his beloved loch amidst a burst of bluish flowers he had noticed the previous day. Careful not to harm their stalks, he ducked, hoping the flowers' blue would provide camouflage. He patted the damp soil in appreciation, curling his bare toes into the comforting coolness. Inhaling the lovely silver mist, he became one with everything, hoping his hiding would be successful.

Around him, shouts and laughter echoed through the mist as Hematite tracked the others down. She was close and probably expected him to hide in the loch as usual. To encourage her expectation, he tossed the bon tree pip he still carried into the middle of the loch where it landed with a satisfying splash.

Softly laughing, he sank lower, his belly pressed against the scratchy stems, and remained still. His hearts raced with anticipation. Had he finally outwitted his best friend? In the light breeze, the mist grew thicker as it did every day. Confident of his camouflage strategy, Cerulean became lulled by the flowers' spicy scent.

The thick stems, nearly as blue as the flowers that crowned them, bounced in the breeze against his shoulders, a hypnotizing rhythm of thumps. Soothed, he closed his eyes. One flower stalk bumped his shoulder in a riotous solo. He stiffened and peeked over his shoulder.

Hematite playfully wiggled the stalk to hit his shoulder. "Got you," she whispered, her eyes pools of laughter.

"How?" he whispered, his palms up in disbelief. "How do you *always* find me?"

She raised an eyebrow in playful mockery. "My element, unlike your water, is a unique combination. Mist and rocks. That makes me stronger...faster...*better*." She covered her mouth to silence her laughter.

"That's cheating." He huffed.

It wasn't really cheating, but his disappointment at being caught so quickly made him claim it as one. They all had advantages. His was in the cerulean waters of the loch, and Clay's was on the rich soil. Still, with her element swirling everywhere, it did give her an unfair advantage.

She touched a finger to her pointed ear, signaling him to be quiet lest he give away her location. With a mischievous grin, she faded into the mist and returned to the game.

He sagged into the flower bed. What would it take to survive in the game longer than she did? One of these days, he would outlast her.

Moments later, when Hematite sprang on Clay in ambush, his connection with the springy loam that he stood on helped him easily outrun Hematite's outstretched arms. Still, he'd been found, and that's what counted in the game. After Hematite found the last survivors, the giant game with all the young Firth ended and Cerulean, Hematite, and Clay gathered under a great bon tree to lunch on fruit. They spent the rest of the day dancing among the song trees that surrounded their loch, swimming, and mischievously stalking friends in the mist and inciting joyous terror in them.

When the cool evening winds cleared the moisture from the air, they touched hands and parted with the familiar saying, "Remember us," as if tomorrow they would have outgrown each other.

Returning home to his family song tree, Cerulean curled up beside his mother on a large branch. "Why do we always say 'Remember us' when we part with friends?"

Her gentle smile and cozy coral glow filled him with warmth. "It's a tradition," she said, rubbing his head.

He frowned and gazed out over the dark forest. The soft, colorful glow of clustered Firth families dotted the canopy—Firth he loved. How bad would things have to be for him to forget those he cared about? It was an oddly dry night, and with the lack of mist, the stars above shone brightly through the long, curling leaves of their tree. "Something would need to be awfully wrong with me to make me forget my friends. If someone started saying it for no reason, can we change it to something less ominous?"

She smiled. "We are caretakers of Lenglood. We must remember all the forms of life we are responsible for."

He snorted. "We sing to them all every day. I'd have to be really forgetful to not remember them."

"It's deeper than that." His father climbed down from his high perch and joined their cuddle, wrapping his long, lavender tail around them. "The phrase also carries a warning about the Day of Reckoning, when all things will be torn asunder and all remembrances lost."

Cerulean groaned. "That's just a myth. How could that even happen?"

"You're right, it's probably not real," his mother said, giving his father a stern look.

"He asked, and he's old enough to know the truth." His father nodded at Cerulean. "But don't worry about it. It's been talked of for millions of revolutions and probably will be for another million."

Cerulean gaped. "You're that old?"

Laughing, his father shook his head. "No, not quite. My point is there's no need to worry about it. We don't really know what it warns of. The ancient song trees taught the first Firth to say it, and now, like your mom said, it's tradi-tion."

Cerulean frowned. If something was that dangerous, shouldn't they, as caretakers of Lenglood, try to prevent it?

His mother pulled him closer in a side hug. "We can't prevent what we don't understand, dear. Go to sleep. We'll join you in your dreams." She grinned. "Maybe tonight will be the night you master your chords."

Cerulean chuckled. *Not likely.* His parents had taught him in his dreams every night since birth, and he had always messed up the final complex chords. Someday he'd master the full awakening song for the trees, but not tonight.

TWO

S everal revolutions passed, and Cerulean grew in both stature and curiosity. During the day, he played with his best friends, but when the world grew dark, his curiosity overtook him. Nestled in their warm nest filled with soft lochweed, he smiled at the shifting hues of his family's glowing colors as they reflected and merged on the walls of their nest. Was every planet as beautiful as this? He pointed up through the leaves. "How do we know the stars are other worlds?" he asked his mother. "Have any of us traveled there?"

"No," she said, smiling and unwrapping the fish both his parents had cooked earlier. "We're quite happy here on Lenglood. Everything we need is here."

He reached up, flexing his fingers as if he could grasp the stars. "But it's possible? I could go if I wanted?"

His father frowned. "What would happen to Lenglood if we deserted her? What of the song trees and the other animals?"

Cerulean sighed and plopped cross-legged into the base of their nest. "Right." He could never leave Lenglood or his loch. He couldn't even go half a day without the joy of splashing in its waters. Another possibility hit him. "Could the Firth from those worlds visit us?"

"I suppose, but they might not be Firth." His mother handed him an entire cooked fish. "They might be other forms of life."

"Like what?"

"The oldest song trees say their ancestors were flown here by the Song Makers."

"You mean older Firth?" he asked, biting off the warm fish tail and slurping it down.

"No, other beings that exist no more."

He put down his fish. "They all died?"

"No one knows, but they are no more."

"That can happen? A whole group of beings can disappear? We failed at taking care of them?" His hearts filled with despair.

"No, of course not," she answered, hugging him. "You're always so full of questions. No one knows anything about the Song Makers except that they lived at the dawn of Lenglood before the Firth." She shrugged. "Maybe they flew off to another planet?"

"And left the song trees behind?" He shook with fury at the thought, then realized he had considered the same journey moments ago. But *he* would never leave the song trees alone.

"If they left, it would be hard to take full-grown trees on a journey such as that."

"I suppose. But I would never abandon them."

"Thus, we stay," his father said. "We stay strong, and we sing, and we remember."

***

The next day dawned milky-white as usual, the world fresh and frothy with morning dew. Fog swirled around Cerulean's legs as he trailed the loch's edge, cautious that at any moment, Hematite might spring at him. A long, drawn-out scream ripped through the fog, and in his terror, he lost his footing and slipped into the water. Sodden and cold, he struggled to stand, searching for the cause of his fellow Firth's terror as the water swirled around his legs.

Another scream curdled the morning, dying with a horrible gurgle that sent chills down his tail. Unsure of the danger, he crouched within the waters, trusting it to camouflage him. "Hematite? Clay?"

A flash of reddish-brown whipped through the fog to his left.

Spinning in the water, he called out, "Clay? Was that you?"

"Ceru—"

"Clay? Where are you? What's wrong?" His hearts raced as he splashed to the bank and extended his hands. "Where are you?"

He shouted so loudly that the nearest song trees froze in their swaying and held their collective breaths. So much for staying hidden from whatever was out there. But even with the trees holding still, he had trouble seeing Clay in the thick mist.

From every direction, shouts and screams poured forth in a chorus of terror.

"Clay," he screamed and risked his camouflage by stepping onto the soaked bank. Instantly, his mind fogged, and he fell back into the water.

"Cerulean!" Clay's arm nearly caught him, but he stumbled over his own feet, his eyes wide with confusion.

Why was his friend suddenly so klutzy? Clay stood on the soil, where his corporeal form should be strongest.

Clay babbled, "Where... I can't... Ceru—"

Cerulean sprang from the water and grabbed for his friend's hand, but his fingers closed on themselves. "Clay!" Clay's hand evanesced into a reddish-brown mist and dispersed into the fog. Cerulean grabbed for his friend's shoulder, but his arm had now evaporated.

Clay froze, gaping at his dissolving body.

"No!" Cerulean shouted, but his friend's body wisped away until only his terrified head and torso shimmered before him.

Tears streamed down Clay's face as he mouthed, "Remember us." His red-brown essence merged with the fog.

Shocked, Cerulean fell back into the water. A cacophony of wails and moans drifted around him like endless rolls of thunder. On all sides, the song trees wheezed in agony as their branches stretched down toward their Firth familiars, but as tall as he stretched, he couldn't reach any of the branches from the loch.

"Remember us..." the fog whispered as it rolled around him.

"No!" He sprang from the loch, ignoring the instant wooziness that gripped him. He raced toward his song tree, yelling for his parents, for Hematite, for anyone. Every step on the solid ground fell sluggish as if the grasses were draining him of vitality. Still, he pressed on from the lake toward his tree. His breath became gasps, and his footing unstable. He glanced down as his blue feet began to shimmer and become transparent. "No!"

Fearful of disappearing as Clay had, he spun around. Remembering the power of his element, he raced back to the loch, falling in face first as his feet became unstable. He dove deep, twisting to run his hands down his legs, terrified to find them dissolving in the blue waters. As his hand slipped past his ankles, he touched gummy flesh that hardened under the water's coldness to his usual thinly scaled texture. He still had feet, but was it safe to surface?

The mist that had always nourished the Firth had somehow turned against them. It still wafted above his beloved waters as it always did. His chest burned with a lack of oxygen. He loved this loch, but he couldn't survive for long within its depths.

The burning in his lungs built. Against his will, his legs kicked, and he broke the surface of the loch, gasping. He treaded water, terrified that his nose and ear tips would begin to soften, but they didn't. Splashing and shouts came from his left.

"Cerulean? Help!"

Hematite! He swam through the waters, racing to the bank. He found her hugging herself, her silvery essence barely holding its form in the mist. She was of the mist and stronger against its betrayal than Clay had been.

"Cerulean!"

He grasped her hand and pulled her to him, his arms enfolding her. He kissed her wet head in gratitude and tugged her deeper into the safety of their sacred waters. "I thought you were..." He couldn't finish. "What's happening?"

"I don't...know." She panted. "Everyone's...disappeared. I...I thought I was the last one."

"But why?"

She shrugged against his chest. "I don't feel right..." She began trembling.

"You're fine. Somehow, our loch is protecting us."

"*You*, maybe, but I'm Hematite, a combination of earth and mist." She clung tighter to him. "I can't feel my feet," she sobbed.

"We're safe in these waters."

But her legs, intertwined with his, were dissolving—her warm form losing shape and swirling into the water around his legs.

"Save me," she begged as if he had some power she didn't. As if he wouldn't overturn the planet to do so if he could.

He shielded her with his body as she sobbed; her tears streaming down his chest merged with the lake. He stared as the tiny droplets plunked into the water. "I don't know what to do," he whispered. Then he shouted to the mournful song trees above, "Help us! Tell me what to do!"

But the trees only dropped a scattering of filmy leaves onto the water as if they, too, were crying.

Her legs were completely gone, and her arms were dissipating from his lower back. Her giant, golden eyes met his. "I don't want to die, Cerulean."

"I can't lose you." He pressed his face into her neck, breathing her into him. "I love you," he whispered.

Her entire body dissolved in his arms until all that remained was her lips against his lower ear lobe. "Remember me, Cerulean. Remember us..."

And she was gone.

He stood in the water, trembling with fury. "What is this?" he screamed. "Why?"

There was no one left to hear him but the song trees, and they had grown silent.

THREE

At first, Cerulean shouted, searching for other survivors until his throat became so raw it burned when he cupped his hand and drew water to his lips.

"Remember us, remember me," he called out.

No response.

He closed his eyes, imagined the energy of the other plane of Lenglood, and by the time he opened his eyes, he had shifted to it. He stood frozen in horror at the lack of organization. The once clear lines of connection the Firth had so carefully nurtured now ran jagged and haphazard. Overwhelmed by the buzzing of the strange, unhealthy static, he fell to his knees. *No. It can't be.*

The entire dimension lay in ruins, and he had no idea how to fix it.

Cerulean returned to his regular plane and tried to sing, but his damaged throat lacked effectiveness, so he resorted to humming. Without the vibrant colors of his family and friends, everything was monochrome, and the mist engulfed him in its silvery sinews. After endless dawns of humming, he grew as quiet as the song trees, passing day after day surrounded by the endless gray. Even his beloved loch became so dull it no longer matched his Cerulean glow.

He swam laps around the loch, kicking in frustration at his watery prison. But fear of dissipating like the other Firth kept him within his watery confines. As he circled, he tried to call up Hematite's face, her silvery scales, golden eyes, and the way her lips had curled in mirthful mockery whenever she scared him, but she seemed a distant dream as if her memories had evaporated with her. It was like losing her all over again, and he pounded the water in a fury.

He lost all sense of time, day and night, and mealtimes. When hunger drove him, he drank loch water and ate raw fish. The uncooked fish disgusted him but not enough to overcome his fear of leaving the lake to cook it.

His throat healed enough for him to sing for the song trees, but his solo contained none of the depth and richness needed to wake his friends. Regardless, he sang every morning, willing his throat to mimic the multitudes of lost Firth and save the trees from their apathy.

The song trees remained silent.

After several evenings, a wondrous idea blazed in his hearts: Maybe, just maybe, he was not alone. Perhaps other Firth had survived in their elements, living on parts of Lenglood too far away to hear him. Perhaps they sang their morning song on the other side at different times so their voices would never be united for the trees. And maybe, if he sang all day, he'd end up singing in unity with other survivors.

Excited to have a purpose again, he sang an entire day and night, his hearts burning with the possibility of the trees whispering back to him. But, as the following dusk added its blue murk to the silver mist, the song trees remained silent.

His hearts broken, he sank to the bottom of the loch. Only its cold depths soothed the burning frustration festering under his scales. Before, he had held onto a deep ember of hope that somehow, somewhere, other Firth survived. That they couldn't have all deserted him, leaving him alone with no parents, no family, or friends—to fend for himself.

The finality of the Firth's extinction infuriated him. If he were the last, he would fight oblivion and become their memory keeper for as long as his sinews allowed. He stomped into the shallows, sat so that only his head and shoulders were exposed to the air, and smashed his fists into the water. "Hematite," he shouted, his fists smacking the water. "Clay." *Smack.* "Lavender." *Smack.* "Coral." *Smack.* "Rainbow." *Smack.* On and on he went, listing every Firth by their glorious color, straining to remember their expression, their laughter, and their love.

This recitation of names became his morning ritual, the only thing that gave him any sense of the passage of time. Every morning as the sun warmed the swirling mists, he shifted into the other plane of Lenglood and checked the energy balance. But nightmarish broken energy lines emanated from the trees, and his hearts raced in the panic that his own cerulean glow remained the only color present.

He had failed. Until the planet was back to normal, he couldn't risk leaving his element and evanescing, because if that happened, he'd have deserted the trees as he'd told his parents he'd never do. Sighing, he returned to the normal plane where his failure didn't flash around him in all directions.

He never ventured fully out of the loch. Whatever evil had possessed the mist that fateful day now seemed over, but he couldn't be sure without risking death. He'd seen no animals other than the fish. That horrible day had left his planet empty of all conscious life except himself and the drowsy fish.

And if he kept eating the fish, soon he'd finish them off and starve to death.

***

Every repulsive meal of raw fish became a countdown toward his impending starvation. The bereft trees remained nonresponsive as if already dead. Yet their nubby buds still transformed into soft, curled leaves, and later, those same leaves fell into his loch to float upon his waters until they browned and dissolved.

He yearned for Hematite's frightening but fun antics, Clay's wild bursts of energy, and cuddling in the nest with his parents. The only interaction he'd had today was the fish nibbling on his legs as if begging to be eaten as to escape their painful existence.

He'd failed his world.

Why had he survived? *Why me?* And why the fish? What about the sacred loch had saved them? He wandered into its shallows and sat on the silty bottom so that only his head rose above the surface.

Once, the Firth had lived all over Lenglood, but if they had survived, he would have sensed them by now in the other plane. There were other sacred places, all with unique energy resonating from them since the dawn of time. Since the time of the Song Makers.

He looked up to the trees. They had once sung of these special places. Try as he might, he couldn't remember the words. Hematite had said something once about the magnetic qualities or electrical qualities of certain areas like the loch. About the rarity of the lighting springs that fed it. But if that were true, why hadn't it saved her?

Tears trickled down his cheeks. This was *not* how he'd wanted to outlast Hematite.

Her good-willed teasing played through his mind. *My element, unlike your water, is a unique combination. Mist and rocks. That makes me stronger...faster...better.*

"I wish you had survived instead of me. You'd know what to do." He wrapped his arms around the air in front of him as if hugging her again, but no warm arms hugged him back.

He stood and studied the quivering branches of the song trees. "Why me?" he shouted up at them.

They remained silent.

"Why won't you wake up?" he yelled.

Again, no response.

He released a long groan of frustration. Why was he mad at them? This was *his* responsibility. Unless he was going to just sit in the loch until he died, awakening them was the only purpose that remained to him. The fish that fed him wouldn't last forever. And when he starved to death, there would be no one to hear his final breath of "Remember us."

His father's words echoed in his mind: *We stay strong, and we sing, and we remember.*

"I can do this," he insisted to the careless fish.

There must be a way his voice could work as many. He waded closer to the nearest grove of song trees, watching as the water rippled around him. Could his voice be like that? Rippling over itself to get the sound of many voices? He turned toward the steep cliff that lined one edge of the loch. Could he create an echo? Taking a moment to calm and center himself, he swallowed his roiling emotions and began to sing.

At first, his voice wavered. It was so alone, so singular. Then, his voice echoed back and sounded like many Firth. He sang louder.

Let this work. Please.

The sun rose high, and a deep vibration reached his ears. The trees had always started off their mornings with overtones before words. Hearts racing, he sang louder. *Yes, it's working!* Something hit his arm, and the sound stopped. He spun to see a druizy fly hit his arm and fall into the water. A second later, a fish greedily snapped it up.

"No..." he sucked in a ragged breath, his chest suddenly hollow with grief. The druizy fly had made the sound, not the trees. His voice had done nothing. Beside him, the fish circled as if still hungry. Wait. He hadn't seen an insect since the morning of the vengeful mist. How had that fly survived?

He swam the circumference of the loch, discovering several other young flies and a swarm of their larvae near one shore. Had the loch saved more life than just he and the fish? Would the fish live on?

He shifted to the other plane. The song trees' energy remained jagged, but new energy crackled in the loch—insects and amphibians. Nothing to carry on a conversation with, but definitely more life than there had been before.

He returned to his normal plane and searched the shallow's tall loch plants. As he leaned closer, his movement wafted pearly white eggs floating in small clusters attached to the stems. The eggs must have been on the surface or clinging to loch plants, not deep in the loch as he had been in those fateful moments, and still, they had survived. Inside each one wriggled black larva, one of which popped out as he watched. He grinned. "Watch out for the fish, my friend."

He gazed at the bobbing eggs. Wait. Did that mean he only needed to touch the water—his element—to be safe from the mist? And if so, how far could he push it? Could he simply be wet and still be safe on land?

Shivering at the idea of risking it, he turned back to the loch grasses, thrilled to have new neighbors. At the top of one stalk, a more mature fly specimen perched, drying its wings. Despite being fully out of the water, it remained solid. Cerulean raised his hand and touched it, afraid he might be dreaming. The fly spun, whipped out its razor-sharp tongue in warning, and flew away.

He watched in amazement as it flitted through the misty air, solid and healthy.

He furrowed his brow at the swirling grayness and waded into the shallows. His hearts raced at the risk, but if he were only out for a few moments, that might be safe. He had briefly run onto the land that horrible day, right? He closed his eyes and jumped into the mist, pulling up his feet to be momentarily out of the water.

As the deliciously warm air enveloped him, he grimaced, expecting the worst, but he only fell down with a splash. Nothing horrendous had befallen him.

So, was the mist no longer dangerous? Or had it never been the problem, and something else had happened on a planetary scale? Whatever that thing was, the loch protected him and the other life within it. But why couldn't it have protected Hematite, even if water weren't her element?

Frustration boiled in his veins, and under the water, his hands fisted. She had been *right here* in the loch with him. What he would give for just a few moments with her or to watch a final moon rising with his parents. Just a hug and a few answers. He had been a mere podling when they had disappeared. How was he supposed to figure this all out on his own?

We stay strong, we sing, and we remember, his father had said.

"We also shift!"

All animal life on Lenglood could shift between the planes, but only the Firth used that ability to care for the wellness of others. Animals of Lenglood—Firth included—were less firmly of this world, less solid, because they traveled throughout all of its planes. Maybe that lack of solidity made them extra vulnerable to whatever had happened?

He dared pull himself up to sit on a half-submerged log but kept his legs in the water. The gentle movement of air about his torso delighted him. To fully dry his upper body, to feel the mist swirling about as an old friend and not a ravenous monster pulling him to pieces made him sigh deeply and tilt his face toward the sky. A fish jumped beside him, and he gazed down at the water upon his wavering reflection. His body was taller and leaner, his face more like his father's. How much time had passed?

Now fully grown, desperate for connection with others, and with no idea how to revive the trees, was there any reason for him to hold on? He sat there all day, stubbornly searching for a way to improve his situation—a way to save the trees.

As the night closed in around him, he stared up at the stars through the branches of the silent song trees. If only his child-self had been right about other Firth up there. He couldn't do this on his own.

FOUR

The next morning, out of habit, he recited the names of all he remembered. As he called out Hematite's name, instead of punching the water, he released a huge, rattling sigh, so deep and full of anguish, it traveled up from his toes to escape.

As his breath shot out, a slight shimmer of silver like the glitter of Hematite wafted in the air. Eyes wide, he reached out to touch the first Firth color he'd seen in ages. As his hand brushed through the shimmer, it vibrated like the tinkling of her laughter when he'd sprayed himself with bon fruit juice. The color collapsed into liquid and streamed into the loch. He stared at the water, as cerulean as his name, swirling and mixing with the silver shimmer that had escaped him. He scanned the loch. Throughout the water, small droplets of hematite color glittered like teardrops.

"Hematite?" Desolation tore at his innards. The lake remained as silent as the day they had all dissolved. "Hematite!"

The song trees bent closer as if they too yearned to reconnect with their lost friends. But the trees had lost their voices, as he had lost his people. He was now losing his mind if he thought Hematite would somehow burst from the waters.

That glimpse of her essence tore open memories of her dissolving from his arms while the screams of his people echoed around him. He spent the next few days sobbing and thrashing in his watery prison. He called out for survivors, but he really didn't expect an answer. He was alone, and, unless the trees awoke, he always would be.

***

At first, Cerulean's discovery of the living insects and amphibians had given him new hope—he wouldn't starve. But the endless sloshing around his loch, eating raw fish, and never again talking to another Firth or seeing their luminous colors tortured him. Firth had extensive lifetimes, and he dreaded this mundane, purposeless existence.

We stay strong, we sing, and we remember.

But to what end? He couldn't save the trees, and who was he remembering for? Would it be best to forget and let himself fade away like the other Firth? His internal despair seemed to leach through his scales into the water. The loch's bright cerulean hue faded to dingy gray, and even the fish swam sluggishly.

He poured all his willpower into the recitation of the names and singing to the trees before lapsing into a daze. He remained so still that fish slept in his shadow. When hunger struck, he'd pluck the closest one from the water. "You'll thank me for this," he'd mumble, and squeezing his eyes in disgust, he'd take a bite. *I'm trying to stay strong like you said, Father.*

Too tired to move, he now recited the names in his mind, though that began to blur. Time slowed, and he had no idea how long he existed like that.

Remember us. Remember us...

The voices of his past called, but he found he could scarcely remember himself, his name.

He no longer cared.

A flash of red in the gray sky jerked him from his daze. Could it be Clay? No, this was not the incandescent color of his people. He swam closer and closer to the shore, minding only the brightness blazing overhead. Bright, fiery red streaked high above the mist, followed by a thunderous roar. He stood in his watery prison, as the color streaked across the sky until it landed somewhere beyond the song trees. Mesmerized by the vibrant color, he waded across the loch, following the red streak's trajectory toward the distant trees.

A sudden wind, caused by the passing red streak, whipped through the trees, blowing long curly leaves around his damp body. As he mindlessly yanked them away, his toes stubbed against something hard. Impossible, since the bottom of his loch was soft and silty. He froze, gripped by fear.

He stood on the solid bank beside his loch.

Solid ground, out of his element.

Hearts racing, he gasped for breath as loud noises rose behind the forest where the red blur still highlighted the trees. What could be happening? The wondrous color pulled him another step forward for curiosity's sake and to protect the forest. What if the red was a meteor and burnt his beloved trees? But his scales were now nearly dry. His mind had grown woozy, his body shaky. He stared at the water's edge and back at where the red blur had disappeared. Back and forth, he turned, desperate to investigate but unwilling to risk the memories he held of his people, and his chance to save the song trees.

He turned back to the loch. He would always choose his people.

The deadly silence that had smothered Lenglood since the Day of Reckoning blew away with the sudden wind. With roaring sounds like thunder, the red light lowered to the ground. Then, strange, distant chatter snapped him from his mental fog. He yearned to investigate the newcomers but didn't dare travel far from the loch.

The visitors stayed. Strangely, the new creatures seemed oblivious to him and his beautiful haven. Their heavy footsteps snapped fallen twigs and branches beyond the tree line, but they never came too close to the loch. Still, whenever their sounds drew closer, and distant Firthoid silhouettes appeared under the trees, he instinctively submerged for safety.

They had to possess the intelligence to travel the stars, and he trembled with excitement at finally having someone to converse with. He yearned to see their bright color again, but fear of dissolving kept him in his sanctuary.

His favorite, misty dawn hours remained quiet, so he guessed they didn't rise to greet the morning. That allowed him to continue his usual morning recitations without attracting attention. Still, he yearned to see what they were doing beyond the trees. To meet them. To see if they possessed the same colorful glow of his fellow Firth. The landscape had been so dull without that bright, luminescent glow.

The sash of red across the sky upon their arrival had been like a mere nibble of food to his starving soul. The urge to see the true colors of sentient beings burned within him so greatly that even the cool waters offered no comfort. And yet, despite his loch possessing the strongest magnetism of all the geological features on the surface of Lenglood, they continued to remain oddly blind to it. If he wanted to experience their colors, he'd have to risk leaving his life-saving waters.

One day when the creatures were far away, he tested the land's safety. After soaking himself, he stepped onto the grassy bank and waited for his feet to feel gummy or his mind to become confused. To his amazement, he remained stable and solid. He achieved six steps before his racing hearts overwhelmed him, and he ran back to his sanctuary.

Every misty dawn, he tried.

He had forgotten how to walk on land, and each unsteady step brought back the horror of his legs' gummy sensations eons ago. His fear of dissolving or losing the memories of his people drove him back to his watery haven.

Each new sunrise, he again risked it, desperate to see colors other than his own cerulean.

On his tenth excursion, he managed to climb the grassy bank, traverse the field of wildflowers, and enter the dappled shade of the song tree grove he had called home. It was horridly silent—no singing, no creatures of feathers or fur flitting from branch to branch.

Treading quietly, he reached his family's song tree, with its one branch looping all the way to the ground as if embracing them upon every return home. But his home was as empty as his hearts.

Nothing remained in the branches of their sleeping nooks or their nesting cloths. Here, his parents had taught him to climb. They had sung him to sleep under its curling green leaves and had entered his dreams to teach him the harmonious chords of Lenglood. How could everything he loved be gone? Sniffling, he plunked his buttocks onto the ground and leaned back against his old, silent friend. "You've left me nothing..."

Sobbing, he looked up at the twisted leaves. He rubbed his palms through the long grass, desperate to feel some connection to the land he had abandoned that day. Something jagged scratched his palms.

Digging through the tangled grasses, he yanked free a few pieces of broken pottery his parents had used for cooking. The clay remained parched and unaffected by his dry fingertips. Trembling at the memory of cozy meals with his parents, he rubbed his too dry fingers over his brow.

His thoughts jumbled, and Clay's confusion that day on the shore echoed through his mind. "No."

He sprang up, grasping the shards to his chest as he raced toward the safe wetness of his lake.

As the cerulean waters rippled around his waist, he ducked below the surface. With one hand clutching his family's broken cookware, his other hand explored his toes and ear tips, confirming he was still in one piece. Lungs burning, he rose above the surface and panted for breath. The mist swirled around him, mocking his fear.

He needed a safe way to check the other nearby areas. Dousing himself, he wrapped in soaked lochweeds and raced to other families' homes. All were in an achingly similar condition to his own tree, yielding only broken pots and bowls.

With the pottery, he created a shrine to the Firth on the shore opposite the strange noises. While he rearranged the tall lochweed protectively around his shrine, the first creatures appeared. Strange, fleshy beings with short tufts of hair walked stiffly upon the land as if Lenglood's soil was a dangerous beast, not to be trusted. They carried hard objects that bleeped and hummed, and when they turned in his direction, he silently sank into the water and remained out of sight.

They did these strange marches through the land for days, and he had to return to quietly reciting in the morning lest he drew their attention. They puzzled him with their nonsensical activities. But they cloaked themselves in color, and for that, he loved them.

At first, their colors confused him. His mother had said those that live among the stars might not be Firth, but he'd never expected that intelligent beings could live without emanating vibrant kaleidoscopic colors. Yet the proof stood before him, bumbling around on his planet.

The only Firth he'd ever seen who lacked such a glow had been when one of the elders had died. He'd been shocked by her dull, gray-green scales. Later, he had been even more shocked when his mother explained all Firth were that same gray-green if one focused on their scale color, rather than their glow.

But these new creatures wrapped themselves in various layers depending on the weather and changed these colorful layers daily. Only their tufts of hair remained consistently the same color—black, brown, or auburn—but those were not a glow that pierced the mist with vibrancy. Still, he cherished their presence and the muted colors they returned to Lenglood.

They stayed away from him and his loch, but he kept an eye on them. Nearly a full revolution passed. Every morning, after his recitation of remembrance, he shifted to the other plane to check his progress with the trees, but he always found jagged and static energy.

To his amazement, the new creatures were invisible there as if they only existed in the one plane. He'd assumed all sentient life crossed the planes as the Firth had, and the remaining animals of Lenglood still did. The more he learned about these beings, the more his worry grew.

about how to maintain harmony with these strange creatures roaming his planet.

SIX

One murky morning, a screeching shattered Cerulean's recitation. The screamer had no need of breath, either. He froze in horror then spun about, expecting the trees and grasses and the rest of his world to evanesce like that other terrible morning. He couldn't catch his breath.

From within the forest, the new creatures' shouts joined the cacophony. He rose from the water, terrified they were dissolving as his Firth had. He barely knew them, but they now lived on Lenglood, and he yearned to protect them.

The top of a song tree shook. *Are they finally waking up to help me fix this? Can they prevent it this time?*

The song tree toppled, crashing through the other trees and landing with a violent thump that shook the water where he stood.

"What?" he whispered. How could such a thing happen?

Ducking underwater to soak himself, he sloppily wrapped himself in lochweeds then raced toward his fallen friend. Peering out from behind a great bon tree, he watched the creatures whoop and holler over the fallen giant. On either side lay the wreckage of its brother and sister trees as their branches sought to break its fall. Panting for breath, he sickened. The creatures grinned as if the toppled primordial colossus had been a danger.

They had done this? They had purposely destroyed one of his few surviving friends?

Fury burned in his veins as they attached metal cords and used a metal monster to drag his slain friend through the undergrowth, adding insult to injury. "Remember us," he choked out as the dead, gentle giant was dragged away.

Tears streaming down his face, he hid behind the bon tree and shifted to the other plane. Light bled from the ground where the song tree had stood. The surrounding trees' energy was more static-filled than ever. He stumbled to the seeping light, holding his palm to the soil, mumbling the few words he remembered from his childhood participation in the elder's death ceremony.

It wasn't enough.

Shaking with fury, he somehow managed to return to his wet sanctuary.

Remember us.

The lost faces of his parents, Hematite, and Clay, flooded his mind. He buried his face in his palms and sobbed. He should have died with them that day. Remembering served no purpose except to bring him greater pain.

The horror of the song tree crashing against the ground and shaking the water kept him awake all night. Firth had no natural predators, and he'd never expected another animal to attack himself or his friends. If he couldn't wake up his friends, how was he to protect them?

In a fury, he soaked his body, wrapped in damp lochweed, and strode toward where the fleshy creatures lived. He had never gone this far, but they had a way of making it clear where they were. He burst through the other side of the forest into a burnt grassland. In the huge circle of dead grasses sat the monstrous hulk of metal they had arrived in. The moonlight of Lenglood's larger moon glinted off its many curves. Around it lay multiple, small domes made of a material he'd never seen before. The creatures had planted the domes around the ship as if it had laid strange eggs over the burnt field.

He shouldn't have come. This was impulsive and dangerous and not exactly improving his mood. Still, he couldn't ignore that his friend's body lay unattended and stretched across the charred field.

He scanned the settlement for danger. His large ears flicked at the incessant buzzing of druizy flies. Nothing else moved. He crept close to the ship and risked a peek through an opening. Inside, the new creatures were all prone, sleeping in the monstrously unnatural shape.

He returned to his slain friend.

Keeping the toppled song tree between himself and the ship, he wailed and lamented its death. The color-clothed creatures opened their ship, murmuring in fear, and stared at him as he sang his sacred songs. After dripping a few precious drops of loch water onto his lost friend, he hurried off to hide in the far end of his lake.

The next day, the creatures marched with their strange bleeping devices, and he sensed they were searching for him. Their uneasy gait and constant scanning of the periphery with their strange contraptions betrayed their fear. He marveled that they studied their contraptions more than the beautiful world around them. It was as if they could only trust their experience of the world through their equipment. Fortunately, their equipment was oblivious to his existence.

As the sun grew higher, they stumbled about, getting closer only by accident. One of them began to peel the layer of color off his upper body and tie it to his waist. Soon, the others began to do the same. Underneath, they ranged in color from beige to dark brown. They wandered about, startled by the whistle of breezes through the reeds, the swirling mist, and the darting, buzzing flies.

Ever since he had sung for the dead tree, they seemed terrified of their surroundings. He observed their strange antics all day, but they never caught onto his presence.

As the sun drifted lower, they untied their old skin layers from their waist and put them back on. They were pathetic creatures, barely vibrant. How could he ever protect the trees if these creatures had no sense of the sounds, colors, and harmonies of Lenglood?

He dove into the loch to refresh his wetness and followed them home through the small woods to their clearing. They seemed to have accomplished nothing all day, acting like lost children in a new, scary world.

Curious, he climbed a bon tree whose broad branches gave him a clear view of their settlement. They cooked outside around fires like his parents had, and his stomach growled for the comfort of a fire-cooked meal. A lone woman with a swollen belly walked around the trunk of the dead song tree, touching each spot where they had sliced it up into smaller segments. Her sad gaze lingered on every detail of his fallen friend until the others called her to eat.

Afterward, they all retired to their ugly ship. As they fell asleep, he considered their prone forms. Could he do as his parents had done for him? Could he enter their dreams? Did he want to risk that when they had slaughtered a song tree?

Torn between annoyance and pity, he remembered the dreams his parents had given him of the harmonious ways of Lenglood. He recalled the soaring choruses of Firth voices that balanced the planet.

As the last Firth, he lacked the harmony to revive the song trees and maintain the planet himself. If these brutes were going to remain on Lenglood, he had to ensure they somehow transformed into worthy guardians, and, so far, he was not impressed.

He could protect the land of his people by teaching these new beings to appreciate it. The possibility of accomplishing this warmed his hearts, but he had no idea how to carry it out. Should he formally contact them, or would they destroy him like they'd fallen his song tree comrade?

The next day, his hearts thumped wildly against his chest as he wrapped in wet lochweed to leave. An odd dread filled him, and he ran into the forest toward the creatures' dwellings, asking the silent trees for comfort. He didn't expect words, but the trees were still living. Perhaps they heard.

As he got to the far edge of the forest, he slid to a stop and hid in the undergrowth. A large group of the creatures strode noisily along with their tool that had killed the other song tree. They approached the trees and slowed their steps, peering about fearfully.

Cerulean called in warning to the trees, but they remained silent, accepting their fate. "You may be mute, but I know you still live," he whispered up to the trees. "I need your help to save you."

The trees remained quiet as the new creatures started up their lethal tool.

Desperate, he clambered up a nearby tree and hid in the leafy branches. He began to sing on behalf of the trees, but they couldn't hear him over their tree-killing contraption.

As the machine drew close to the trunk, he shrieked a high-pitched sound that even these brutes could perceive. Below, the creatures stopped and looked up in terror. Several waved smaller gadgets into the branches in a threatening manner. He shrieked again, and they turned off their tree-felling tool.

Praying that his cerulean was similar enough to the leaf color to camouflage him, he began singing.

They gathered near his tree and looked upward in fascination.

Pond scum! What had he been thinking? Now the dangerous creatures knew where he was hiding. He could shift to the other plane and escape back to his loch, but if he left this plane, they'd no longer hear his voice.

Still singing, he eyed the branches of the nearest tree and sprang from branch to branch, hoping to make it appear that the tree itself was intoning.

After a while, the group below conferred. Looking upward, they slowly pulled their awful device away from his friend's trunk.

He warbled on about gratitude and friendship before leaping to the next tree to wait in silence. They didn't restart their device. He leapt from tree to tree until he reached the loch, and then scurried down the far side of the trunk and dashed to the water.

Cerulean sighed with relief as its waters clothed him in a blanket of wetness. He rested that night with joy in his hearts. He had *finally* saved someone. Maybe he did have a purpose, after all.

Cerulean awoke with a mission: to learn more about the creatures so he could effectively teach them to live harmoniously with Lenglood.

Thrilled to have a project, he completed his morning recitation of Firth names in the pre-dawn darkness. When the sun broke the horizon, he used the swirling mist for cover and ventured to the periphery of their settlement. Staying within the trees or tall grasses that had regrown near their ship, he observed and learned, periodically returning to his loch to soak in the water before drying out.

He began learning their language and absorbing every detail he observed. They were humans and considered themselves masters of everything, and rulers of all life. Yet, every night as he observed them through their ship windows, they became vulnerable as they slept. Oddly, even if they woke, they never fully saw him, even when looking at him directly. For whatever reason, perhaps because of how firmly planted they were in this physical plane of existence, they noticed him more in their peripheral vision, but then dismissed their glimpse of him as a dream.

Gaining confidence in his ability to avoid detection, he snuck in and touched their brows while they slept just as his parents had touched his brow to enter his dreams. Unlike the Firth, human sleep was long and naturally dream-filled and bizarre. Their sleep stories were often non-sensical—so different from the beautiful, intricate stories his parents wove into his dreams every night.

In their dreams, he whispered about the beauties of Lenglood and shared stories of the song trees and the Firth. He always gave them a bathing of cerulean light before he left, hoping if they experienced real color, they could find their own colors and leave their old ways of control behind.

But while awake, they still believed they controlled everything and dared to declare Lenglood their planet of Pentrox IV. Only the littlest ones accepted their home as a playmate rather than something to tame. The children warmed his heart with their games of chase, so similar to what he and his friends had played. And, they climbed the youngest song trees.

Once, one fell asleep, nestled in a branch, and Cerulean had returned to the loch and cried that he'd never again cuddle in a nest with his family, despite the fact that now he was old enough to have his own podlings. No, there would never be podlings on Lenglood again. He was the last Firth. His people were as distant to the humans, who had never directly met a Firth, as the Song Makers had been to the Firth.

Given the adults' hardened sense of ownership, he doubted that directly challenging it would end well. He allowed them the sense of ownership but whispered beauteous tales of guardianship rather than ownership in the twilight hours of their sleep. The changes were painstakingly slow and subtle.

"Clear this jungle for homes" became "What about tree houses?"

"Those resources will sell for a lot of coinage" became "Perhaps others could benefit if we shared the unique biodiversity of this place."

It was far from ideal, but Firth were long-lived, and he burned with memories of a balanced Lenglood. A Lenglood where every life form was remembered and life was harmonious.

Cerulean could gift these dreams to them, but they lacked the ability to shift visions to physical reality. They needed an attitude adjustment during their waking hours. He pondered how to help them with that as he walked back to the loch to replenish himself. The lochweed wrapped around him had dried enough to scratch his thighs.

Hoots and hollers came from his left. He ducked into a patch of the same blue wildflowers as those he had hidden in ages ago from Hematite. It the distance, three children threw mud balls at each other, giggling with delight as it plopped onto their bare legs. *Their children love it here.* Small and innocent, they rolled on the mossy ground and danced in the mist, unlike their fearful parents.

He climbed a nearby bon tree. After asking the tree's permission, he picked a juicy bon fruit and tossed it down to the children. They all jumped in shock and looked up into the tree branches.

Well-hidden, he sang them a song.

Wide-eyed, they stared up at the tree. "It's a spirit," one of them whispered.

Cerulean tossed down another fruit, careful not to hit them, but they scattered, teasing each other about their fear as they all ran as fast as they could toward the ship.

Laughing, he decided since the children were the most open and Firth-like, he'd spend his days teaching them. He began leaving the children presents after they had done something kind. A flower one morning. A shiny rock the next. These were parts of Lenglood they could cherish and appreciate.

The kids called him Ghost and made up silly stories about him. Their parents weren't sure what to believe, having once seen his lamenting shape over the dead tree.

In the children's dreams, he began passing on the stories of his youth. To keep from scaring them, he always made it seem like human dreams, though gradually, they became more and more accepting of Firth-like dreams. As always, he let his cerulean light shine in their dreams, hoping it would awaken their own light. He'd whisper, "Remember me," before he left each sleeper.

They never did.

They knew he existed, but they had no idea he visited them every night. Somehow, his colors didn't show up on their sensors, and the adults began calling him Ghost as well. He liked the name as it reminded him of the silvery droplets of Hematite's essence that had stayed with him. Like she had somehow stayed with him, he would stay with them until they learned to respect the planet they had chosen for their home.

EIGHT

Cerulean sat on the sun-warmed bank be-side his loch, brooding as he stroked the broken pottery shards of his people. Caught between two civilizations, his existence was the final lone note of a song, tenaciously lingering in the hope that the humans would somehow, impossibly, join the lost melody.

A sudden metallic clanking made him shrink against the ground in fear. *Not the trees again.*

With great care, he replaced the broken pot in its hidden sanctuary, and then, as he stood, he shuddered, energetically hit with the sudden silence of extinguished lives. It only took a moment's check-in on the other plane to identify the horror. While mosses and grasses never sang, their existence created a steady hum that he only now noticed for its absence.

Running to investigate, the cloying scent of crushed and mangled lives flooded his nostrils, making him retch behind his tree. The mosses and grasses had been ground to pieces in the jaws of their vehicles. The ignorant humans had torn up an entire field. That night, he wailed for the mosses, the grasses, and the clueless humans.

The humans came out and began arguing with each other, and to his surprise, some of them argued for the Ghost of Pentrox IV. But not enough of them. The next day, they dug up another field, and he nearly screamed aloud, giving himself away, as they erased the nameless flora from existence. Devastated, he sang again that night over the mangled, bare soil. Numb from horror and too drained to think properly, he stumbled back to his wet sanctuary.

When he toppled down the bank and into the loch, even the cold waters couldn't refresh him. He had seen too much death and the erasure of too many colors from Lenglood. His tears mixed with the water, and he considered never surfacing. A flash of red streaked above the dark surface of the water. He shrank back, picturing the arrival of more humans and the utter destruction of all he knew. But the color didn't whip across the sky. It splashed in his loch.

He circled it from below and then edged away and surfaced. In the darkness, he would be invisible to the humans because they didn't seem to see colors that well. Blinking, he swam closer. The vibrant, red glow, bright enough in the black murk of night to drown out its unseen source, lacked the brownness that Clay had possessed. The splashing became frantic, and as he swam closer, he spotted a small girl within the vivid light.

How could this be?

She splashed helplessly and began to sink.

He dove toward her sinking body, scooped the little thing up, and surged upward to surface. She coughed water all over his face and shoulders, but that wasn't his concern. Despite her Firth-like glow, she was firmly of this world, whereas he wasn't. She was difficult to hold. His arms kept passing into her as if she weren't there, and for a terrible moment, he thought she was going to disappear as Hematite had.

"Don't go," he begged, trying his human speech out loud for the first time.

She stopped fighting him and gasped. "Are you Ghost?"

He laughed with joy. He hadn't been truly seen and addressed in eons, but he also feared she'd pass right through his arms and sink into the depths. "Yes, if you want. Let's get you safe."

He swam toward the shore, constantly adjusting his arms to hold her. When they reached the bank, he helped her stand in the shallow water.

She stared at him, wide-eyed. "Are you a monster?"

Being unfamiliar with that word, he gave his ear an anxious tug. "I'm a Firth, and this is my home." He couldn't stop staring at her glow. Surely, after all these years, he would have noticed a glowing human on his visits to their village. "How are you red?"

She looked down at her drenched clothing and furrowed her little brow. "I'm not red." She didn't see it.

"You're glowing the color red."

"Is that bad?" She pushed her wet hair from her face and began wringing out her clothes.

Was she a new creature and not truly human? "You're a human child, right?"

She laughed. "No, I'm six and an *adult*." She waited as if it were some sort of test. Or a game.

"Okay." He was lost. "Can I call you Red? Or do you have another name?"

"Red?" She scoffed. "Why do you keep talking about that color? I'm Cinta."

"Cinta," he repeated. "Thank you. Can you please tell me why your people are destroying the vales of Lenglood?"

"Huh?"

"The humans tore up the grasses and mosses. They killed everything." Tears pricked at the memory of their screams as they were extinguished.

Her eyes grew round with wonder as she studied his face. Reaching up, she touched a shaky finger to his cheek.

He held her gaze. "I'm real. I'm not a ghost, and you are killing my planet."

She bit her lip and looked ready to cry. "The grass cried when they dug it up. I told my mom, but she said I was telling stories."

"You heard them?"

She nodded. "Mom said it was because I heard Dad tell the story of the tree crying."

"No, that was real." He held her tiny hand in his. "I'm real, too. And I need your help."

"Okay. I don't like it when the plants cry."

"Good. Come back tomorrow, and I'll teach you to swim, and we can talk more." He eyed the stretch of song trees between his watery home and the human settlement. "You better go before they get worried and come looking for you."

"I'm six, not a silly fool," she said, grinning. She turned and ran back through the trees and into her development.

As the red girl ran under the song trees, he thought a few of them sighed.

The next morning, he was sunning on his log at the far side of the loch when a red glow told him Cinta approached from the tree line. She wore a strange, small piece of cloth, carried another thicker piece of cloth, and now stood on the shore with only her toes in the water as if amazed to have found his lake.

He dove from his log and swam up to greet her. "Hello," he said, throwing in a human wave for good measure.

Her jaw dropped, and she began to back away.

"Cinta, wait. What's wrong?"

She froze. "Are you Ghost?" she whispered.

He frowned. "Yes, we met last night. Don't you remember?"

She shook her head. "I wasn't here last night. I went for a walk under the trees."

"You may have walked under the trees to get here, but you were definitely in my loch last night. You were upset over the dying plants and almost drowned."

She gaped at him as if amazed at his knowledge of her.

"You don't remember meeting me?"

She shook her head and wriggled her toes in the water.

"That's odd." Frowning at her lack of remembrance, his gaze bounced from her red glow to the loch. The water helped him keep his memories and stay intact. Was it possible it had the opposite effect on her?

"You remember being upset about the dying plants, right?"

She nodded.

His heart surged. "I heard them crying as well."

Her big, brown eyes studied him, then she plopped down on a tuft of grass and dangled her legs in the water. "They want to keep killing the grasses to put in other plants that grow food." She stroked the tuft of grass. "I asked if we could just eat the grasses, and they laughed and told me I was *too little to understand*." She pouted.

His eyes narrowed. Too little. Yes, he'd been right. She was a child, though why the youngest was the only one to understand made no sense to him. "Were you born here?"

Her eyes widened. "In the grass? I wouldn't think so."

He laughed. "No, on this planet. On Lenglood."

She scrunched up her face. "I was born here, but that's not what it's called."

"Hmm." He'd need to begin singing that name in their ears at night. "Are they going to kill grasses today?"

She nodded. "That's why I walked this way; to get away from the screams."

"Hmm." *No, your mind somehow remembered to come back.* "What would stop them from doing that to the field?"

She pursed her lips in thought, then sighed. "Nothing will stop them. We need to start growing food, or we'll starve."

"You need food." He looked around the lush landscape. How could they be smart enough to travel between planets and not know about finding food? "Okay, wait right here."

He left her standing in the shallows and raced off into the woods. A moment later, he returned with two different kinds of fruit. "Go, give these to your mother, and come back tomorrow."

Only after she left did he realize he had risked gathering the fruits without first wrapping himself in wet lochweed. Such carelessness was inexcusable. He must take better care of himself. He alone carried the memory of his people.

NINE

Cerulean yearned to follow Cinta home and see how her mother reacted to the gifted fruit, but he couldn't easily travel among the humans in the daylight. He had already been too careless. He swam impatient circles in his loch, waiting for the sunset. As the sun crossed the sky, the horrible grind of the human machinery began again beyond the trees. *What now?*

Wrapping himself in lochweed, he rushed through the growing shadows of the trees. From the tree line, he watched in horror as the humans destroyed another beautiful vale. If he didn't somehow speed up his teachings, they'd destroy too much for Lenglood to ever recover. He had to fully impress them with Lenglood's natural bounty.

He waited until nightfall and found Cinta's home by finding her red glow in the small window of the home made of strange, water-proof material the colonists had brought with them. Checking through the window for the building's layout, Cerulean quickly shifted planes, took a few steps forward, and then reappeared inside her home. Humans used doors, but he usually couldn't activate their doors from the outside.

Unlike the Firth nests, human homes were extravagant and housed many adults and children together. From their common scent, he guessed everyone within each unit was a big family of sorts. He found the two adults closest to Cinta and gave both the identical dream song of how to find and prepare the fruit.

As he finished up the end of her father's dream, Cinta rolled over, and her eyes fluttered open. Cerulean froze as she mumbled something incoherent, and then her eyes drifted shut again. Had she seen him? To be seen was to be a known, and he trusted Cinta, but he feared alerting the adults that their legendary Ghost snuck into their homes. Trembling, he shifted to the other dimension, fled their home, and ran the entire way back to his loch.

He awoke to find humans running through the woods, searching for the fruit tree. He smiled. If he could get them to live in harmony with Lenglood's natural bounty, he just might train them to be good stewards.

At night, he taught them in their dreams as his parents had taught him, telling them stories of his Firth, and how to appreciate each plant. He began to think of the humans as his children.

They learned well as long as they weren't afraid. He also found they disappointed him often, and he would return to his haven, fearing his plan would never work. Every time that happened, Cinta would reappear, renewing his hope with her growing love for Lenglood.

She never mentioned having glimpsed him that night. While it broke his hearts that she never remembered him, she was always quicker to trust him and quicker to laugh with him. Just as he could walk on the land for a while, she could enjoy swimming for short periods. But whatever they discussed during their visits was forgotten. Even so, he suspected their friendship had influenced her because she had begun wearing primarily his color, though she never knew why she liked it. Each time they met, she instinctively remembered how to swim and walked lightly on the grasses.

"Cinta, why do the others never come down to my loch like you do?" he asked her one morning.

She shrugged and splashed water at him. "I don't think they know about it."

How was that possible? He splashed water back at her, but not with his usual enthusiasm. "But they walk by it often enough."

"It's like a ghost lake, Ghost," she teased. "*I* know it's here and can see it, but it's shimmery and different than other lakes. It's not on any of our maps in school, you know." She grinned, and her red glow lit up his world. "And it messes up our tech to get anywhere near it. This whole area around it has weird"—she scrunched up her face, trying to remember—"electromagnetic fields?"

"Hmm. This area is special. Maybe your red helps you see it? It's like you've shifted to become more like me."

She frowned at her dripping shoulders. "Shifted how? Am I going to start growing scales?"

He snorted. "No. When I first taught you to swim years ago, our hands kept moving through each other, and it was hard to touch."

She furrowed her brow and grimaced. "That's weird. It didn't happen today."

"Right. That's the kind of change I meant. You've shifted somehow. Maybe someday, the others will, too. And when they find the lake, I can splash them, too." Laughing, he drenched her.

Sputtering with hiccups of joy, she swam in a circle to face her village. "You'd be okay with that?"

"Yes. As long as they're nice. Bring the ones who shine with their own colors."

She wouldn't remember that, but he always talked to her as if she would. He could inspire her in her dreams to bring them along. To create human stewardship of Lenglood, he needed to risk talking to more of them.

But she kept the loch secret until the song tree blossoms bloomed and then brought a friend with a deep-purple color. When they returned another day, her purple-lit friend also had forgotten him. And so, to the humans, he remained a ghost, not Cerulean.

When Cinta grew tall and began blushing and laughing about boys, he found himself curious and sought the ones she talked about out. He spoke to her cherished boys at night, teaching them in their dreams, so that whoever she chose would love this place the way she did.

He was not always kind, though. One boy she liked, Dante, was mean and cruel to the song trees. When he climbed the tall, wet rocks on the west side of his lake, Cerulean knew it would prove deadly, but he did not intervene. He didn't want mean and cruel humans living and reproducing on his planet, and he did nothing to save the boy when he fell. He did cry later, but for Cinta and the boy's family. All life should be cherished.

His fondness for Cinta grew, and those few hours every morning, when she came to swim in his loch, were the most precious hours of his day. He yearned for someone who could remember his existence. And then he recalled his gray period when he had no one. He had never expected to be seen and talked to again. Perhaps it had not been a curse for him to have survived. He still held the memories of his people, and he was grateful that humans had arrived and had started to develop colors of their own. Perhaps he could make good stewards of them after all.

Above him, the song trees rustled in the breeze. He sighed. Their rustling of leaves was the only sound they'd made in eons.

"Whatever I've accomplished, I've still failed you, my friends."

The trees remained silent. Maybe he wasn't the best steward to be teaching the humans.

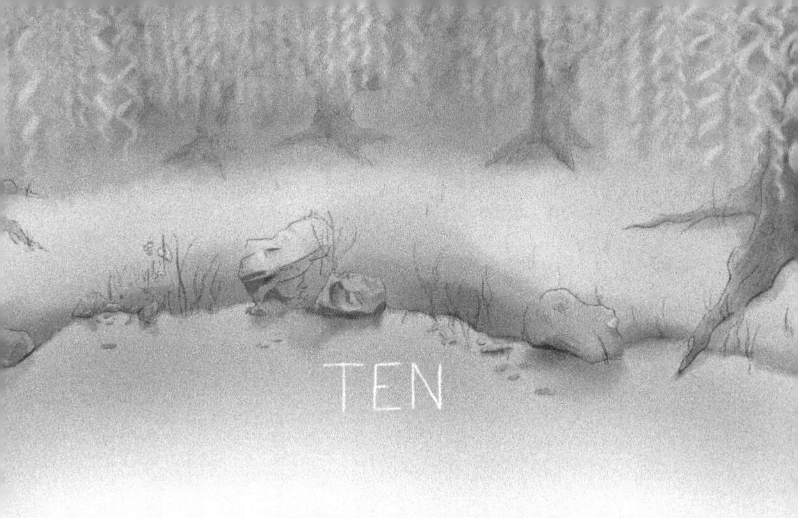

TEN

The only thing that differentiated one day from the next was his forgotten interactions with Cinta and all the humans' dream-lives. He yearned to be a part of something: a two-way friendship, a family, or a community. Instead, Cinta and the humans developed deep relationships among themselves, from which he was excluded.

He considered meeting Cinta away from the lake, but he still feared the humans may not like knowing they shared the planet. They had grown to respect the other life, but it was not conscious or threatening in any way, and they remained more fearful than the Firth had ever been.

As much as he wanted Cinta to remember him, he feared meeting her outside the loch might somehow undo all his work. And so, he remained alone. Cinta did not. She eventually chose well and married Fin. Cerulean found it amusing that she asked Fin to wear blue for their wedding as if she wanted a bit of him there.

Years passed. Cinta and Fin had six children and raised them all to cherish the land and sing to the trees. All their children had colors, and Cerulean secretly named them Starlight, Jen-tree, Russet, Plumvine, Aquamarine, and the youngest he named Bonflower after the sweetest nectar on Lenglood.

Other children began to be born with col-ors as well. The humans began to self-regulate themselves, sending away humans who would not respect their planet and enjoy its beauty.

They played more and even visited his loch. He spoke with many of them. None ever remembered him other than a being of their dreams and tales—the legendary Ghost who left do-gooders special gifts overnight.

He watched Cinta grow old, her hair silver like hematite, and her dark eyes full of more wisdom than he'd known humans could possess. She stumbled down to his lake one morning, an utter wreck. Her eyes were red, and tears stained her cheeks.

"My dear Cinta, what happened?" He rose from the water and touched her arm.

She drew back and stared at him. "Who are you, you cerulean ghost?"

He laughed, despite himself. She was so close to knowing who he was, but never quite got it. "I'm your longtime friend who watches over you and your family. And you never remember me, but that's okay."

She nodded as if that made perfect sense. "Then, I guess it's good that you're here."

"Why? What happened?"

"F—Fin..." She drew in a shuddering breath. "Fin died. Do you know him, too?" She brushed tears from her eyes and trailed her hand in the water. Red droplets glistened into his loch, reminding him of Hematite's tears eons ago.

"Yes, I did. I'm so sorry." He stepped closer. "Would you like a hug?"

She nodded, and when he held her, it was as if she remembered him. Almost. She melted into him and sobbed. It was too much like Hematite, and he stiffened at the memory. Cinta wouldn't be around forever, but he couldn't think of that now.

"What do you need?' he whispered.

She sobbed. "I loved him so much. Now that he's gone, I feel like I've lost my best friend. I told him everything. No one else in my life is like that."

She shares everything with not just Fin, but with me as well.

Today, she had lost Fin, but Cerulean lost her every day. As he choked back his own tears, he managed, "I know, love. I know."

She sniffed and wiped her face dry. "Do you think I'll ever have that kind of sweetness in my life again?"

He looked into her deep brown eyes, so different than Firth eyes and yet so similar. He brushed a strand of hair behind her ear. "You have your children and grandchildren."

"Yes." She was so close; her breath warmed his chest. "But something is missing. It's like... I don't know, like a song I can't quite hear or something."

He looked up at the silent song trees and back at Cinta, the obvious answer to his problem. How had he not seen it earlier? He grinned. "Yes, you're right. Maybe we could do something about that. Want to try?"

She gave him a puzzled look and then shrugged. "Sure."

"You see those trees above us?"

She nodded.

"Those are song trees, but they no longer sing, because they're so sad."

"I can understand that," she said, sniffling again.

"My beautiful Cinta Red, you understand so much more than you know. That's why I'm wondering if we both try, maybe we can wake them up."

"Try? Try what?"

"Singing." He cocked his head as she considered it.

"Okay."

He taught her a Firth song that no one else but he had sung for eons. It was simple but strong like the long curving branches of the song trees.

I sing because I can, and the day is good.

We sing because we can, and the day is good.
The day is good because we sing.
Love, love, love.

As they sang, the trees began to sway ever so slightly, and a low humming came from above.

"Hear them?" He sprang up and down, splashing them both in his excitement. "Keep singing!"

She laughed tiredly and continued to sing. Another tree began to hum along. Why had he never thought to teach her to sing this song before?

They sang until the sun was high in the sky. Exhilarated beyond belief, they grew quiet and basked in the arboreal chorus.

"My dear Cinta, may I show you something?" he asked.

She nodded, and he wrapped his arms around her and shifted to the other plane, trusting that her having color meant she too could travel there. A moment later, they both gasped.

In both planes, they stood in the loch with water up to their chests. But this new-to-her plane glowed with incandescent light he hadn't seen since his childhood. The static that had haunted his dreams was gone, and the jagged, torn lines of energy had been restored to their pristine glory. He sighed in delight. "Isn't it lovely?"

She nodded, too overcome for words.

"Thank you, my love." He kissed the top of her head. "I could never have saved them without you. I wanted you to see what we've done and not just hear it."

"What is this place?" she asked, wide-eyed.

He considered her language and understanding. She was smart, but he'd learned over the years that human brains struggled to understand Firth concepts. "I believe you'd call it another dimension, one where we can more easily see the energy connections and maintain the heart of Lenglood."

"It's...stunning."

"Yes, *now* it is," he said, grinning. "But I must get you back."

She gave a slight pout of disappointment, her dark eyes filled with reflected light. "If you must..."

"I must. But we can return another time." He hoped they'd return many times; he had so much to still show her.

His hearts leapt with the success of her entrance into this plane. There were hundreds more they could explore together. He had only mastered a few, given how young he was when the others all died. The two of them could have a grand adventure. And if she could enter the other planes, perhaps her children and grandchildren could as well since all of them had inherited their own inner glowing color. He shifted them both back. "I believe now that we've awoken them, you'll soon hear the song you crave."

"Thank you, Cerulean. It comforts me to see there is more than I ever imagined in this world. Maybe..." She gave him an embarrassed grin. "I'd like to believe my beloved Fin has moved on to a beautiful place like that."

"Yes. I hope all those we've lost now reside in a place like that, and they're all making music and playing together somewhere."

She nodded and squeezed his hand tighter. He led her to the shore and helped her climb the bank. As she stood with one foot in the loch and one on the bank, she turned to him. "Your voice was the song I needed." She smiled and wiped her damp eyes. "I won't remember you?"

"No, but I'll be here nonetheless, waiting. And when you return, I'll remind you of our friendship."

She kissed him on the cheek and turned to leave. As soon as her foot left the water, the old pain returned. He was now as forgotten as if they'd never met. She turned and gave him a strange look as though to say, "Why is this strange creature so close to me?" but she did not call out in fear. She just hurried away. But as she did, he loudly hummed his song for her.

ELEVEN

The next day, Cinta did not come, and Cerulean was beside himself with worry. He'd spent the night checking on all her adult children in their own homes, making sure they were okay after the loss of their father. He swam back and forth. Should he risk walking into the growing village during the day? No, he couldn't risk undoing his work and scaring them all. That night, he ran to her house and found her asleep in her bed, her breath rattling in her chest as if it were her last.

"No," he begged and scooped her up. "You can't die. I still need you. I'll have no one."

His wetness dripped onto her face, and she began to awaken. She'd be terrified to find him holding her. He bent to put her back onto her bed.

She grabbed his arm and opened her eyes. "Who are you?"

"Your friend, Cerulean." He smiled through his tears. "Your people call me Ghost, but you know me as Cerulean."

She narrowed her gaze. "What are you doing in my house?"

"You didn't come to the loch today. You've come every day since we met, and I was worried you were...ill." He blinked back tears. She was not ill, but she appeared to be not long for this world. He could feel her fading like Hematite had faded, but she was still here physically.

"Then you better take me to the loch," she said sternly.

"What? Why?"

"Take me." She looked a bit scared but not of him. "It's where I want to be. Hurry."

He turned and carried her through the shelter and out into the night. As his feet padded across the moss, swirling the endless mist, a song rose on the air. He stopped and whispered, "Do you hear that? The song trees..."

She coughed. "They're beautiful, but I like another song better."

"You do?" How could anything be better than the song trees? They were glorious eddies of song.

"Yeah, I heard it the other day when I was walking home." Her dark eyes glistened with yearning as if the cherished song still pulled at her. "It was such a lovely song."

He laughed, and it was his long-lost laughter of the bubbling spring. "The song I taught you? You remember?"

She shook her head against his shoulder and coughed again. "I don't remember you singing. It was just a melody. Like humming..." She frowned and then hummed it.

"That's the Firth song I taught you." He had hummed it after she was out of the water. She had held onto a memory of him! As he strode past the mosses and under the song trees to his loch, he again sang the song to awaken the song trees. She had carried a direct memory of him. Not of his color, but his song. His hearts warmed, and he nestled her a bit closer to his chest. He still hadn't entered the water, so if she survived her current frailty, then this memory of him would survive. "We're here," he said, unsure what exactly she wanted.

"Take me in with you. Could you do that? I've never actually gone into it, and I'd like to before I die."

He sucked in a shaky breath. "Yes," he whispered, "but wouldn't you rather be with your family?"

She shook her head. "No. All life on this planet is my family. This water is somehow my favorite place, and yet I've never swam in it."

He smiled at her, but his tears blurred her so that only her red glow shined clearly. "Okay, but it might be cold. It's nighttime."

"It's okay," she whispered and patted his cheek. "For some strange reason, I trust you."

He chuckled. "Okay, Cinta Red, in we go."

He strode into the loch, its depths full of his memories, his people, him. As the water grew deeper and passed his waist, its coldness touched her back. She turned toward his warmth, and he held her higher. "You sure?"

She nodded against his chest, "It's time..."

Tears stung his eyes. "I don't want you to go, my friend. You'll be gone forever like the others, and you won't remember me. It'll be as if we never even met."

As she shook her head in disagreement, her dark eyes sparkled beneath the folds of her skin. She patted his cheek, now damp with tears. "My people believe in an afterlife. After we die, we review our whole life and learn from it, and then pass on to a beautiful land."

"I don't understand."

"When I look over my life, I will memorize every moment on this beautiful planet. And I suspect you will be in parts of it, right?"

He grinned. "Maybe a few."

She gave him a tired but warm smile. "Then, I'll know. And I'll remember."

"But you're saying this in my loch. You won't remember what you've told me or remember to memorize what you see."

She smiled. "I've seen your shadow in my dreams, my love. And it always told me to look for brightness and kindness, and love in life.

When I look over my life, your cerulean light will shine like a beacon, because that's what you've been."

"But how could you know that?"

"Because I'm already gone..."

He stiffened. *Gone?* No. But her red light hovered above her body, not within it.

"Cinta Red, remember us," he called as she shot up into the night, leaving him alone in his loch. Tears streaming down his face, he closed her eyes and kissed her forehead. "Good luck in your new world. Remember us, my love."

He somehow managed to get her to the shore and lay her on the softest bit of moss. The trees sang more loudly than before, and soon, the whole village would be out to see who was singing. Fixing Cinta's nightgown, he sobbed at the absence of her beautiful red glow as the song trees dropped their large white blossoms onto her. He arranged them as beautifully as he could and sang the Firth songs for the dead.

Returning to the lake, Cerulean considered his options. He, too, was tired and wanted to rest. But if he died, his people would be gone and forgotten.

Above him, the ancient trees leaned over the loch, their curling leaves trembling as their song resonated throughout the starlit night. "My dear friends, it has been so long without you, but now I fear it is my turn to grow silent and no longer contribute my chords to Lenglood. But then, the Firth will be gone forever, erased without a trace. What should I do?"

A beautiful, white flower floated down through the air and landed on the water at his chest, and the song trees began singing his morning recitation. All the names of his beloved Firth rang out into the night, and then his name, too.

"We have drunk of the waters where you preserved their memories," their boughs whispered. "The waters will feed future generations. Your stories are in the water and in their human dreams. The Firth will live on."

He gazed upon his beloved loch. The dazzling drops of Hematite's tears, his own bubbling laughter, and Cinta's red sparkled back in greeting. Whispers arose from the depths, the sounds of millennia of Firth playing, drinking, and living. He'd saved all those vibrations?

The trees sang back:

We sing because we can, and the day is good.

The day is good because we sing.

We sing because Cerulean the Firth remembered Us

Love, love, love.

The weight he'd carried since that awful morning slipped from his shoulders and sank in the waters. Bone-tired, he still worried about Cinta's family. He'd always looked after them. "But the humans..."

The trees rustled with laughter. "Are you planning on taking on their memories as well, our friend?"

He chuckled. "No."

"You have taught the humans well and deserve to rest. We will take it from here. We shall sing to the humans that you awoke with your color and love. Lenglood shall continue..."

Lenglood would continue. Something remained of the Firth other than the few shards of pottery he'd collected. The humans loved their planet and had discovered their own colors. The stories of his people lived on, and their names lived on.

He could rest.

Submerging one last time into his beloved waters, he swept his arms toward his chest, pulling the water to himself as if embracing it. *Thank you. May you always assist these new human guardians as you have helped me.*

He surfaced and exhaled all the light he'd carried and was surprised to find not just Hematite's and Clay's, but all the other colors of the rainbow. They swirled around him and spread over the water and the land and the mist, nourishing it as Lenglood had nourished them. "Goodbye, my friends," he gasped, reaching for a final breath. "Remember us..."

Contented that his beloved Lenglood was in good hands, Cerulean soared up into the stars in Cinta's wake. As he looked down one last time, the humans stumbled from their beds and gathered by the loch.

"Listen, Mom!" a child exclaimed. "The trees are singing. Do you hear them?"

"Yes, my dear, I do. It sounds like they're saying, 'Remember us.'"

Also by Branwen OShea

Finding Humanity Series:

The Calling, Book 1.0

The Chasm, Book 2.0

The Cords That Bind: A Liminal Tale From

The Finding Humanity Series, Book 1.1

Acknowledgements

While writing is often a solitary act, the creation of a book involves many. I hope I didn't forget anyone.

Thank you to my children who read every version of every draft, put up with my strange world-building questions, and support me in so many wonderful ways. You two rock!

My amazing editors Trish Johnson and Zen Grabs both taught me so much. Thank you.

For her amazing cover, a hearty thanks to Rai Fiondella, cover artist extraordinaire. You captured Cerulean's grief perfectly and are a joy to work with.

Thank you to all my beta readers for reading the early versions of this: Michelle Fohlin, Jean Gilberte, Karla Johnson, Nur Refai, Samina Refai, Lisa Rockenmacher, and Barbara Sarcia. Your feedback was precious.

Much appreciation to my critique partner Dawn Mancarella, who fielded all my weird writing questions.

Thanks to all my #WritingCommunity friends on Twitter. Your daily support, humor and wisdom is priceless.

And thank you to all you readers who take the time to read Cerulean's and Cinta's story.

About the Author

As a young girl, Branwen wanted to become an ambassador for aliens. Since the aliens never hired her, she now writes about them.

Branwen OShea has a Bachelors in Biology from Colgate University, a Bachelors in Psychology, and a Masters in Social Work. She lives in Connecticut with her family and a menagerie of pets, and enjoys hiking, meditating, and star-gazing. Her debut science fiction novel, The Calling, launched her Finding Humanity series, now three books and growing. She also has an adult paranormal cozy, Werewolves, Chocolate, & Pigeons releasing in 2026.

In a future ice age, Northern Haven's expedition team is desperate to find other surviving humans. When they emerge from their subterranean refuge, they discover a new civilization. The only problem: the civilization isn't human.

www.ingramcontent.com/pod-product-compliance
Lightning Source LLC
Chambersburg PA
CBHW040539170726
48295CB00012B/526